# TELLING THE BEES

NP Novellas:

# TELLING THE BEES

## Emma K. Leadley

NewCon Press
England

First published in the UK July 2023 by
NewCon Press
41 Wheatsheaf Road,
Alconbury Weston,
Cambs, PE28 4LF

NPN021 (limited edition hardback)
NPN022 (paperback)

10 9 8 7 6 5 4 3 2 1

ISBN:

978-1-914953-52-1 (hardback)
978-1-914953-53-8 (paperback)

Cover layout and design by Ian Whates

Editorial meddling and typesetting and by Ian Whates

# One

*'Telling the bees' is a European custom in which bees are told of important events – births, marriages, deaths, departures and returns – in their keeper's lives. If this tradition was forgotten or ignored by the household, or the bees not 'put into mourning' when their keeper died, there would be a penalty.*

*This could be the bees leaving or dying, not making honey, or, the hive collapsing.*

## Lunchtime, 14th August 2035

Sarah had been at work all morning on her farmstead. She'd weeded the multiple vegetable patches, making mental notes of what could be picked and what was yet to ripen. A warm breeze rustled through the greenery as she toiled, carrying a familiar scent of pea vines and herbs.

At lunchtime, she stood up and surveyed her morning's work. Happy in her own company, she walked through the fruit trees, past the compost heap, and rinsed her hands under the outside tap. Whilst the weather was good, she needed to make the most of it and decided on a quick sit down and bite to eat before heading back out.

She was daydreaming about the fruit canes when the doorbell rang, making her jump. She put her coffee down whilst blinking fast to scroll through the external camera footage on her info-lens. The bell was followed by a loud insistent knocking and she frowned; she wasn't expecting anyone, yet they must really want to reach her. *Good thing I'm not out the back.*

She peered through the front door's spyhole to gain a new perspective on this interruption to her normal routine. Her cottage sat on the edge of a small village and visitors were rare, salesmen almost unheard of. And the postman knew where to leave parcels when she didn't answer.

A black hatchback sat on the driveway and standing back from the door was a woman, probably about Sarah's age, glancing round at her surroundings and absentmindedly fiddling with her sleeve. *Sunday best*, thought Sarah, looking at how she was dressed.

Sarah opened the door. "Can I help you?"

The woman's hand flew to her open mouth and she took a moment to speak. "Oh my gosh, Becca. It really is you." Her eyes sparkled, and she grinned widely, stepping forward to grab Sarah's hands. "We never thought we'd see you again."

Sarah moved back, removing her hands from the stranger's. "I'm sorry," she said, "but I don't know you."

The woman stopped as though slapped in the face. "No, it is you." Tears started forming and she scrunched her face up hard, breathing in and out multiple times until she regained control. "It has to be you."

Sarah blinked and darted her eyes to the side, setting the cottage's tech system to record the encounter via her info-lens. With more dialogue and visual data, she could spend time later trying to track down who this was. "Okay," she said. "So, who's Becca? With more information I might be able to direct you to the right place."

"Can I come in? It's not an easy explanation."

Sarah hesitated, thinking quickly about the living room; all the tech was hidden away and there was nothing of any value or interest. "Okay." She stepped back to make room, and the woman walked into the cottage with a slightly awkward limp as she crossed the threshold.

"Oh, this is lovely," she exclaimed, looking round. "So far removed from Becca but still the same recognisable taste." She nodded at the art prints on the wall.

Sarah clenched her fists, which hung at her sides. She shouldn't have said yes to the stranger. And now she'd have to get rid of her, somehow. "So, you're looking for a Becca who looks similar to me but isn't me...?" she prompted.

"You are Becca, you just don't know it. You left me and Blake even though you promised you wouldn't."

"So, who are you, then?"

"I'm... I'm Brea, your girlfriend."

Sarah narrowed her eyes. "And Blake?"

"Your boyfriend." The woman paused, bringing her hand to her mouth. "Oh. Oh god, you really don't recall anything, do you?" The colour in her face drained. "We thought... well, we thought you'd disappeared physically, but we never ever considered you'd disappear mentally, too."

Sarah stared. "Nothing you've just said makes any sense. What do you want from me?"

"We were all happy together until your research became too successful and, well..." Brea looked down at the floor, lost in thought. She snapped her head back to stare at Sarah. "Do you really not remember?" Her eyes flashed with anger.

Sarah reached for her phone in the back pocket of her jeans. It had been there just moments before she'd answered the door but wasn't in its usual place now. She took a small step back towards the kitchen, mentally mapping out the knives, hot sauce, anything that could be a weapon at close range. *No, I'm a farmer, not a fighter.*

"My name is Sarah," she said, jaw firm to hide her nerves. "And I live here, with my nice quiet life. I think you should go." She walked forward resolutely, blocking Brea and forcing her towards the front door.

"Becca, please! We want you back, the three of us together again, our hive mind. We miss you, and both Blake and I need to know what you know. It'll save us all."

"I'm sorry." Sarah closed the door on Brea's heels and collapsed onto the sofa. That had been far too strange and nonsensical an encounter. She looked round, trying to imagine for a moment she was who the visitor had described, but everything was so familiar, there was no way she could be this other person. Her eyes stopped when she spied her phone on the coffee table. She frowned; it had definitely been in her pocket when she answered the door.

She picked up her coffee and took a swig, nearly spitting it out at the unexpected tepid temperature. She decided to brew a fresh one and mentally restart the day. The kettle was just heating up as an alarm flashed across her info-lens in a rapid, syncopated rhythm. With the camera view that appeared, she saw someone wandering around the backyard.

The alarm quietened on acknowledgement. It could have been a lost hiker, Sarah thought, but the timing of it was too much of a coincidence, coming so soon after the random visitor earlier.

Abandoning her coffee, she headed to her untidy little desk in the corner of the living room. She pressed her fingers against the underside of the lip to trigger a hidden switch. The user interface of the cottage's tech system turned on. A keyboard appeared in mid-air and part of the wall liquified into a high-res screen, showing the property from various camera angles.

Sarah's fingers were nimble as she pinched and stretched at the screen to zoom in and out of various bits of the farmstead. It wasn't a big space and she knew every inch, but she wanted to see what, or who, she was dealing with before even thinking about venturing outside.

There! Movement near the outhouse. She zoomed a camera in. Her tiny, songbird-sized drone might draw attention. If someone was creeping around with bad intent, she didn't want them to know they were being watched.

The hairs on the back of her neck rose. She peered forward and pinched out the screen to get an even closer look. A nervous giggle left Sarah's lips: it was nothing, just a few short, midday shadows of the fruit trees moving in the breeze.

A different camera, the one covering the back of the cottage showed a flash of movement. She jerked up straight and stared at the screen. Reaching slowly under the desk, Sarah grabbed the baseball bat she'd taped there in a fit of paranoia. With a flick of her fingers the screen showed views from multiple cameras. Someone was at the back door.

They looked tall, wearing clothing better suited for an office, not a muddy farmstead. Sarah paced the other side of the door, in the kitchen, waiting for whoever it was to do something... *anything.* "Are you coming in, then?" she shouted with a confidence that betrayed her nerves.

The handle pressed down, and the door swung inwards. She took one breath in, one breath out, squared her feet off and prepared to swing the bat. Just as self-defence classes had taught her.

A large hand clenched at her wrist, blocking the swing and pulling her to the doorstep. "Shit, it really is you, Becca."

Sarah jutted her jaw. "I'm. Not. Becca," she hissed through clenched teeth.

"Ah yeah, I heard you talking to Brea through her ear-piece. You really have done a number on yourself."

Sarah flicked through her mental inventory. His voice was low and calm with a fairly generic accent. She was sure she'd never heard it before but hopefully the cottage's tech system would help her identify him, and Brea, later.

"So, you're Blake then?" she asked. The more data recorded, the better chance of a match.

He laughed. It was a warm, low chuckle tinged with sadness. "Yes. But I wish you could remember that yourself. Then you wouldn't have to ask." Blake looked her up and down. "You're looking good, you know."

Sarah's lip curled at his arrogance.

"The three of us were good together. We spent the past few years looking for any sign of where you could have gone. We miss you. We miss *us*. Despite everything, life just isn't the same without you."

His voice trailed off and he stared at his hand, still holding her wrist. Sarah looked, too. Between the knuckles of his index and middle fingers was a small scar, faded with time. She knew what it was, had heard of ex-cons knifing out their biochips on release. She'd probably do that too, were she ever in that position.

She took a step back into the kitchen, squaring her feet and keeping her weight balanced on the back foot, to take a good look at Blake. He was a good-looking guy. Well-groomed and wore his clothing well. A light beard concealed a dimple on one side. No, not a dimple a... scar?

When her gaze reached his eyes she faltered. They were the brightest azure. It was then she knew she'd never met him; she'd never forget eyes like that. They were beautiful.

Blake saw her change stance and softened his grip on her wrist, as though he were taking her pulse. He looked like he was about to cry. "You really don't remember, do you?" he asked softly.

Sarah shook her head from side to side. Partly in reply and partly because a low buzzing tickled the inside of her ear. It wasn't like the occasional tinnitus she suffered, and it droned, like a low-level alarm reminder. This was a multi-sensory noise that grew in intensity until it made her sinuses itch.

"Air," she gasped, overwhelmed. "I need air."

"Okay, let's go for a walk. Show me the life you've built and perhaps some memory or thoughts might come back."

Sarah nodded slowly, wanting to be left alone. She knew who she was, but fresh air would help her feel better and perhaps Blake would disappear as suddenly as he'd arrived.

"You won't be needing that," Blake said, easing her knuckles from the baseball bat and dropping it to the paving slabs next to their feet.

# Two

**Mid-afternoon, 14th August 2035**

Sarah pulled on her footwear and she and Blake made their way across the yard. Despite the afternoon warmth, Sarah shivered, thinking about the strangers and their double act. Blake had mentioned listening in. Was Brea also listening? And if they were all equal, as they'd said, why had only Brea knocked on the front door whilst Blake skulked round the back?

She stalked across to the outhouse, her boots filthy with accumulated layers of muck and mud and hard physical work. Blake kept pace, despite her efforts, and she couldn't help noticing his grimace at the mud that splashed across his brogues and up the legs of his expensively cut jeans.

The buzzing was still there in Sarah's head, but it had faded to more of a background noise, almost like it had settled in place for the time being. She wheeled the barrow of weeds from the morning's labour round to the compost heap and piled on big forkfuls with years of practise.

"Can I help?" asked Blake, indicating the barrow.

Sarah nodded, allowing herself a wry smile as he struggled. After a few attempts at pitching the contents of a loaded fork, he grimaced and handed it back, checking his nails. *Definitely a city-type*, she thought.

She looked round. The routine of the farmstead with its ebbs and flows through the seasons was comforting and stable and she couldn't imagine having a different life.

Blake followed her to the chickens but hung back as they surged forward in a loud, clucking melee in their huge pen. She topped up their water and feeders whilst the chickens pecked and muddied her boots and ankles. Now she had a few moments away from the stranger, she thought about his eyes. They were so uniquely coloured that surely, if she were this Becca, she'd remember them? She shook her head. It was all preposterous. But a memory stirred and flickered, half images that didn't seem to belong to her. A beach where the sea met the sky, so wide you could almost see the curve of the Earth on the horizon. The brightness of the light turned all the blues into dazzling shades of azure and aquamarine. The same colour as those eyes. Where was that beach? She'd been there, she was sure, but when? Perhaps as a child?

Back in the present, her thoughts turned back to the two strangers who were so convinced she was someone else. Blake and Brea were not suited to the rural environment, so by implication neither was Becca. But she'd always known farming, hadn't she?

"So, tell me about Becca," Sarah said, her voice breaking into the background hum as she pointedly looked at Blake for answers.

"It's so bloody odd, seeing you in front of me but hearing you talk about yourself in the third person," he replied. "Becca is the geek of our trio. Neuro-hacking. Able to do medical stuff with brains and memory, all sorts of things that no one else can." He glanced round. "This is never something I'd imagine you'd have, sorry, she'd have, chosen. It's a great place to lay low, this rural isolation."

Sarah let out a long, slow breath. *Neuro-hacker?*

Blake looked at her. "Tell me, how do you know all the tech stuff if you're a farmer? Both Brea and I are impressed with your setup."

She stiffened. "What tech stuff?"

"Come on, security cameras everywhere? Unless it's to discourage sheep rustlers, of course?" He grinned, eyes twinkling.

She realised with relief he didn't know too much about her tech setup. "It came with the place, part of the security system."

"And how did you buy the farm?"

"Farmstead. It's not big enough to be a farm." She corrected. "When my parents died, I bought this with the inheritance money."

Blake raised his eyebrows. "That's a nice, simple tale. Every detail fits."

Sarah glared at him. "It's the truth."

She turned and walked away, leaving the chickens behind and heading to her fruit trees. The apples looked as though they might soon be ready for harvest. Perhaps she should get some help again this year; it promised to be a very full crop.

She realised her thoughts and the persistent buzz was filtering out Blake's words. He'd asked her something and was waiting for an answer.

"Sorry, miles away. What was that?"

"I said, do you make honey, too?"

"Honey?" She looked at where Blake was pointing. A ramshackle hive sat in the far corner. "Oh. No. I've never kept bees." She frowned. The buzzing in her head was louder still.

"So why is your farm called 'Three Bees'?"

Sarah looked round at her land and sighed. So many questions. She turned to the Blake, standing next to her. "Look, I'm sorry. I don't know what to tell you. I'm not Becca. I don't know you and I don't know Brea. I'm certainly not some geeky brain hacker type. I'm a farmer. I have my animals and my garden and that's literally my lot. I can't help you."

13

She fell silent and waited, wanting Blake to disappear so she could get on with her every day, very normal, very predictable life.

He looked around too. "You're definitely Becca. I could prove it with a DNA sample but there's no point, is there?"

Sarah shook her head, her eyes coming to rest on the hive again. The buzzing droned louder, every time she looked at it.

"Look," he said, eventually. "Here's my number. If you remember anything, anything at all, get in touch. Please."

She took the business card, stuffing it into her pocket. Card was such a fashionable thing, she thought: a flirt with ostentation for those who wanted to afford it, when a digital transfer was so much easier.

Blake was staring into the middle distance. He turned. "I, I –" He looked down at the ground, the first time his confidence had waned. "I'll see you again, Becca."

Sarah watched as he walked off, his shoulders slumping, and followed him from a distance until he reached the front gate. A black hatchback waited for him, the same one she'd seen Brea arrive in that morning. A car door slammed and the engine roared. They were gone.

Instinct told her to go investigate the bee hive, but she started shaking, adrenaline levels crashing after the stress of holding her ground, then her nerve, with the two strangers. They weren't threatening, or so she thought, but anything could change. Perhaps she should go and have something to eat and a warm drink. After that, check the cottage was secure and ramp up the security scans. Then, and only then, she could find out if the hive was the source of the buzzing in her head.

# Three

**Early Evening, 14<sup>th</sup> August 2035**

Sarah grabbed a pack of trail mix as she headed back through the kitchen and flicked the kettle on. She needed strong coffee and something to eat to offset her shaking. Today had been weirder than she ever dreamed possible and she needed answers to questions she had only just learned existed.

She picked up her mobile phone, the one that had mysteriously disappeared and reappeared, and laid it on the desk. The minimal data she held on it transferred to her spare device in microseconds, leaving her with a functional new unit and the potentially compromised phone to be destroyed.

She took Blake's card out of her pocket and looked more closely. His name and a number were printed on it, no company or job title. Running her fingers over the surface, she couldn't feel any chips or anything untoward; it was exactly what he'd said it was.

Sarah then turned to the tech system to run recordings of both of their voices for a trace. It gave her enough time to press a new batch of coffee. Its bitterness, offset with sugar, helped her calm and centre her thoughts.

Nothing came up in the databases and Sarah sat, worrying at her lip with her teeth and wondering what to do next. She ran Blake's number and it came up with a match for his name.

Nothing else. It was either a trap or he was who he said, with a standard private number.

She got up and stalked out of the cottage in disgust. It felt like a waste of an afternoon and she was now too wired to focus. Something nagged at the back of her mind, but she couldn't find any clarity in the whirling stream of thoughts in her head.

A walk around her land would do her good. The drone was charged and ready to go and she sent instructions via her info-lens for it to rise up and follow her as she walked the farmstead's perimeter. Looking for something, anything, that might help or give her a distraction.

Starting at the front gate, she moved around, checking the cottage's signalling system was intact and fences weren't broken. Both today's visitors had left easily and she'd definitely sensed a disappointment at her lack of response. But perhaps they were planning on coming back and she wanted to be ready. What for, she didn't know, but a strong, internal urge gave her the impetus to double check her previous groundwork and safety measures.

Whilst walking, Sarah decided to upgrade the security system. Perhaps she needed stronger warnings or more of them in different places. The immediate solution was the fluorescent dye powder stored in the outhouse. It would take her a while but laying it round the borders of her farmstead would give her peace of mind. No one would see it normally, but the drone would pick up its signature glow with its infra-red camera as the powder got walked underfoot. Then, she'd know if there were trespassers and where they were headed. It felt like the old wives' tale of salting a property for protection, only instead of feeling amusement at the thought, Sarah wondered how much truth could be put into it.

The back field gave way to woodland behind and where her land ended at a fence, the trees began. She started to lay the powder whilst her drone transmitted visuals back to her via the info-lens.

She paid them little attention as everything looked as it should. She knew the property and its land like the back of her hand and very little, other than the seasons, altered the view. She changed the drone's camera to show the trail of the powder as she went. It glowed brightly, cutting through evening light. The drone looped round and flew back along the tree line, and Sarah paused the footage, frowning.

Something within the woods was different. She'd barely registered it due to familiarity, but she stopped her work and rewound the recording. It was only on the second re-watch she'd seen a definite glint of something in the trees, on the periphery of the drone's visual feed.

She sent it back for a closer look and anger built as she recognised the flash as a glint off a small, hidden lens, high in the trees and pointing directly towards the cottage. Continuing forward, she and the drone stumbled across a second lens, focused on a different wall of the property.

Sarah stood and looked back towards her home. Despite the outbuilding, there was a pretty clear view of two of the four sides from her standing point. Hands on hips, she mentally ran through the other two sides – was she being watched there, too?

Back in front of her cottage, she paled. Looking closely into the neighbour's land across the country lane, via the drone, she thought she could see another couple of lenses.

Whatever Blake and Brea wanted, they were clearly serious if they were able to plant that sort of tech and have a live feed in such a remote area. Or perhaps it wasn't a live feed at all? Maybe they needed to come and collect the data?

Sarah shivered. She looked around, feeling unnerved. It had been quite a day, and everything just seemed *wrong*.

She headed back indoors, looking over her shoulder every few seconds, and checked all the internal security. Through the cottage's internal system linked to her info-lens, she tested alarms on windows and doors, including the trap door leading to the cellar. In her current mood, Sarah needed to be sure she was as safe as she could possibly be.

Next, she ran through a mental inventory of the property in her head, checking that there were suitably heavy implements within reach from each room, and formulating escape routes for different eventualities.

It was late when she dropped onto the sofa with a sigh, stretching out her arms and shoulders to relieve the tension. There was nothing more she could do. The chickens were safe and fed. She was secure in the cottage, the drone set to record a lap of the perimeter every ten minutes.

She massaged her temples and jaw, thinking a bath would be a good way to relax. She paced as the water poured and, when ready, she sank into the bath's foamy depths, forcing her limbs to relax, her muscles to soften and for the jumpiness to subside so she could feel herself once more.

Sarah started drifting to sleep, her mind filled with disjointed, disconnected thoughts interspersed by awareness of the mild buzzing in her brain. Everything had been fine until Brea had knocked on the door only a few hours ago.

She sat bolt upright, water splashing over the side of the bath. A phone was ringing but it didn't sound like her ring tone. Panic rising, she jumped out the bath, and pulling herself into her dressing gown, looked for the source of the noise. It was her own phone but ringing from an unknown number. Mentally berating herself for not having set it up properly earlier, and for paranoia kicking in, she held the phone cautiously away from her ear as though it could explode. "Hello".

"Hi, Becca. I mean, Sarah. It's Blake."

"What do you want now?" she asked, her jaw tensing again. "Is spying on me from all angles not enough?"

"Huh?"

"Your surveillance cameras, or have you forgotten those?"

"I don't know what you're talking about."

"How did you get this number, anyway?" Sarah's brow furrowed. "Oh, your girlfriend extracted it when she took my phone. Clever."

"Please, Becca. What's this about cameras?"

Sarah hung up and towelled herself dry. She didn't have the mental energy right now. Besides, if it weren't Blake and Brea, who was spying on her? She yawned, exhausted, craving her bed.

She climbed under the covers, checking the house security once more. The mattress was soft and welcoming to her weary limbs and she started drifting off to sleep, only to sit with a start, massaging her buzzing temples.

# Four

## Midnight, 14<sup>th</sup> August 2035

After an hour or so pacing back and forth, Sarah knew she had to face the beehive. It was definitely linked to the buzzing in her head and the persistent sensation was tiring. Conscious of being watched, she took a convoluted route, looking in on the chickens roosting in their coops and checking the outhouse was locked.

She circled round to the fruit trees, mentally working out lines of sight from the cameras. To her surprise, the hive was located in a corner that couldn't be seen from outside the farmstead.

She took out a torch and, with different light filters, checked the hive over. It was old and dilapidated and held together more with flaking layers of once-white paint than structural integrity. UV light showed no body fluids and a fluorescing powder had already been dusted, as a couple of fingerprints showed. A quick scan from the info-lens back to the cottage's tech system confirmed who they belonged to. They were hers.

Sarah rocked back on her heels at the revelation, worrying at her lip with her teeth. She had barely noticed the existence of the hive, so how could she have touched it and not remember being there?

She steeled herself for a further look. If she'd touched it before, surely it meant there was more to discover? The fingerprints were more numerous on one side, petering out as they got lower until there was only one left at the bottom.

Sarah ran her fingers over all the surfaces. Nothing felt out of place, as far as she could tell, just old, splintered wood fragments and paint flakes falling off at her touch. Remembering how she turned on the cottage's tech system, she pushed on the underside of any surface her fingers would fit. Still nothing. Frustrated, she sat back again, looking for anything that might help.

It hadn't been inhabited by bees for as long as she'd lived on the farmstead at least, so perhaps it was time to dismantle the hive. No bees meant no stinging. Gripping the torch between her teeth, Sarah lifted the ramshackle lid and exposed multiple, empty layers. A few bits of old comb and a couple of dead bees were all that was left. Examining the lid showed nothing, even when she used different lights to illuminate every gap and crack.

She struggled to get the lid back in place and with a final shove, it fitted back, but she dropped the torch. From its uneven position in the tall grass growing round the legs, it shone upwards to the base of the hive. The grass touching the base glowed blue, reflecting something.

From the angle she was looking at, the fingerprints on the side resolved into an arrow, pointing to the base. On closer inspection, Sarah saw a concentration of fingerprints in a small area. Her heart leapt.

Lying on the cold ground, she worked her arm into the gap under the hive at the right angle to feel around whilst still giving herself light to see by. Tapping her fingers over the base near the prints, it sounded hollower towards one of the legs. She pushed up and heard a faint click followed by a whirr of a small motor.

She scrambled to her feet, heart racing. After a few moments of walking back and forth on the grass to calm her nerves, she was ready to continue. The trees were still in the orchard, the grass not moving. The night air smelt of the farmstead and if she weren't covered in grass and mud dust, investigating the hive, it would be just like any other evening.

Crouching down, she shone the torch back underneath the old hive. A tiny compartment had lowered to reveal a small transparent cube with something glinting at its centre. The buzzing had quietened; Sarah knew she'd discovered something important.

Whoever – was it her? – had put it there wanted it kept safe and hidden. She could ignore what was happening and go back to her everyday life, but who was she kidding? After the strangeness of the day, nothing would ever feel quite as stable again. Besides, there was a pull, an insistence from her core that she find out what was going on.

Out of a newly formed paranoid habit, she looked round, watching both the shadows and more lit areas of the garden. Nothing moved, and she waited until the drone had completed another patrol circuit, reporting nothing out of the ordinary, before grabbing the little cube. Released of its weight, the compartment tucked itself up again, flush against the bottom of the beehive as though nothing had just happened, down to the aged markings and scrapes that fully matched it to the rest of the base under normal light.

Sarah breathed a sigh of relief and clambered to her feet, dusting off the grass stalks and soil that clung to her clothing. The dirt didn't bother her normally, working with the chickens and the garden, but right now, all she could think about was the curious object in her hand and keeping it clean, so she could get a proper look at it in its current state.

In the cottage, she bolted the door and sat at her desk, putting the cube down and shining the sidelamp on it. She stared at the strange object. A transparent cube, barely the size of her thumb nail in any direction, housed a dense network of pulsing, shimmering gold veins connected by junctions and nodules. It looked like circuitry but at the same time seemed too biological to be electronic.

Sarah didn't know what to do with the sealed cube. Instinct told her the chip was the key. She held it up to the light and spun it on its axis between her thumb and forefinger for a closer look. It was perfectly formed with no chinks or dints, and none of the edges could be split. There were no catches or levers, nothing to get to the chip housed inside.

She stared, frustrated. Made from glass or a rigid polymer she concluded, tapping it, which implied the whole small device had to be fit into a receiver of some kind. What that would look like, or where it would be, was yet another mystery.

Sarah yawned. She was shattered but the buzzing had stopped, and instinct told her she was close to discovering something. She got to her feet to stretch and her phone rang, a startling noise disturbing her quiet contemplation. She put the cube down on the desk and reached for the device. It was Blake, again, and she sighed. She'd really have to block him at this rate.

"Yeah," she answered.

"Hey, Sarah, we were cut off earlier. I know it's late but as I was saying, the surveillance isn't us. If you're in danger we can help you, please —"

Sarah dropped the phone. A message blinked on her monitor, and her heart nearly skipped a beat.

## Storage device detected.
## Scan fingerprint to activate.

The print scanner on her virtual keyboard glowed and she instinctively reached out with her hand, too quickly to procrastinate.

In a split-second, the room was bathed in a glowing pulsing light that changed quicker than she could blink. The cube hung suspended in front of the projector beam from the monitor and a light shone through that illuminated the whole room. Words and images, sounds, even smells, streamed in all directions in a dizzying array.

Mouth open, marvelling at the spectacle, she spun around trying to take it all in. But as suddenly as it had started, it stopped, the cube dropping to the desk. It dulled from an all-experiential mirror ball to its former small transparent cube, cool to the touch.

She stood, unable to move in the aftermath.

"Sarah? Sarah, are you there? Is there someone with you? What's going on?"

She looked down to see her phone, still broadcasting Blake's voice. "Hi. Yes, I'm fine. Thanks."

She hung up and flopped down on the sofa, exhaustion kicking in. She ached to see the cube's content again with an urge pulling and tugging at her, almost viscerally, to see more than she'd glimpsed. It had all been a blur — but it had shown her *something*, no: *someone*. It was her but not her. Was it Becca?

# Five

**2 am, 15<sup>th</sup> August 2035**

Sarah woke several hours later, shivering on the sofa. She rubbed the back of her neck and then rotated her arms to loosen her stiff shoulders.

Full of sleep fog, she realised it was nearly 2 am and her info-lens alarm was flashing. Someone was in the driveway at the front of the cottage.

Sarah jumped up to find her baseball bat. No, wait, a kitchen knife would be better; she knew how to use one at close quarters if needed, didn't she? She hesitated, puzzled, wondering where that thought came from. Mind you, she wouldn't rule out a weird dream after the day she'd just had.

Bat in hand, she hefted it a few times and used the cameras to give her more information. There were two people, climbing out of their car, and moving quickly to her front door, looking worried. Sarah breathed a sigh of relief. She sort of knew who they were and, more importantly, they didn't look armed or about to attack.

Even so, she put the security chain across the door before opening it. "Bit late, isn't it?" she asked, watching them stop in front of her.

"Becca no, Sarah. Wait, we think you're in danger!" Brea pushed at the door and it held on the chain. "Please! Let us in, we can explain."

Something about the furrow of her brow struck Sarah as cute – a random thought to have at this time, she realised. "How do I know you're not the danger?"

Blake stepped into view, hands up. He lowered them in slow, calming motion. "Look, let us tell you what we know and then if you never want to see or hear from us again, I promise we'll go."

Sarah relented. There was something about these two she couldn't explain. She didn't want to trust them but also sensed they weren't lying. And perhaps they could give her more information on the mysterious cube. "Okay."

She let them in and they followed her to the living room. Sarah swept the cube from the desk and pocketed it before they could see. "Drink?"

Without waiting for an answer, she grabbed a tumbler and poured herself a whisky. She downed the measure in one, letting it slowly burn down her throat and revive her tired senses. "Okay, shoot!"

Blake massaged the bridge of his nose before getting up and taking another couple of glasses from the cupboard. He rifled through the freezer and came back with ice for the three of them, decanting them each a shot.

"We took three and a half years to find you," said Brea. She swirled the ice in her glass before taking a sip. A practised habit, Sarah thought. "Yesterday, we rushed over. We were naïve. I…"

"What she's saying, Sarah, is we thought we'd found Becca," said Blake. "Only, you're her but not her. Whoever buried Becca took her deep."

"And… and, if that means you're Sarah forever, then so be it," said Brea, picking at her nails. "But, we didn't plant the surveillance and that means someone else did."

Sarah looked at the pair, frowning as ideas coalesced. The thought of bees – and Blake and Brea – buzzing together sprang to mind. The cottage was called Three Bees and she thought about the hive in the garden. What was it that Brea said yesterday, *hive mind?* What was going on?

"Okay, I'm thinking out loud here," she said. "So, if I were Becca, what danger am I in? Who's the threat? And why?"

Blake and Brea swapped glances.

"It's a long story," Blake said. "Will you humour me for one second?"

"Go on," said Sarah, trying not to sound impatient.

"Before you found the cameras yesterday, have you always felt safe here?"

"Guess so."

"That's good," said Brea, her face crinkling in worry. "But now we've visited, and you've seen the surveillance, we don't think you're safe any more. I'm really sorry. I think we might have caused things to happen, I just don't know what."

"I don't think we can stay here right now, though," said Blake. "Can we go somewhere else to talk this out?"

"How can I trust you?" Sarah frowned, thinking of her soft, warm bed.

"Do you have a choice?" Blake shrugged, a half apology.

"Yes! Of course, I do! I can get you two to leave, take the cameras with you and go back to my actual life. There is no danger. There's no one else here and –" She clamped her hand to her mouth. Alarms on her info-lens flashed an intrusion alert and filled her vision for a few seconds making her want to heave.

"What's happening?" asked Brea.

Sarah paused as she looked through the images being transmitted. "There are people running from the woods and across the back field. Looks like there are either four or five of them. They have guns." She took deep breaths to counteract the rising panic, a dizzy pressure taking over her head. "They shot out my drone, dammit. Who are you? Who are *they?*"

Blake grabbed Sarah by both arms and spun her to face him. "You have to trust us, please. Take a deep breath. And again. That's right. You're no good to anyone, least of all yourself, if you're panicking."

Sarah looked up at him, desperate. She wanted to believe the two of them, that they could help release her from the encroaching nightmare, but how?

The colour of his eyes struck her once again. The smell of salty air and sea reaching to the horizon came back into her mind. After the rest of what had happened she knew it wasn't a coincidence. "Tell me about the beach!"

"The beach?" he looked puzzled. "What do you mean?"

"St. Bees," said Brea. "We went there so many summer days, the three of us."

"Yes!" said Blake, recognition flooding his voice. "Of course! Long sandy stretches and the sea meeting the sky. I remember you, Becca, running out to meet the ocean, kicking off your shoes as you went and just giggling as you paddled."

"St. Bees," whispered Sarah, mostly to herself. "Of course, it had to be." A stronger memory came back. She was there on the beach but not alone. There were two others there... it was enough for now. "There's three of them scouting the yard and outhouse. The others are," she paused, "heading round to the front."

"Other than the front and back door, are there any other exits?" asked Brea. She pulled a small item from her pocket and Sarah backed instinctively away, recognising it as a modified blastgun. Turning back to Blake, she saw he had something similar in his hand.

"There's the coal chute in the cellar, accessed by trapdoor in the pantry." she said. "Although it may be blocked at the other end."

"What'd be blocking it?" asked Blake, inching towards the kitchen. "And where does it lead?"

"It comes out at the far side of the house, on the corner near the yard. I use the space for general storage, keeping the driveway and yard clear. Could be anything in front of the hatch."

"Do we have much choice?" asked Brea, eyes darting wildly. "If they really are covering the exits, we're sitting ducks unless we can escape."

# Six

Parallel bars of weak light illuminated the kitchen from the blinds. Instinctively, Sarah went to switch on the light but stopped herself and instead turned to the pantry.

The door was old and heavy, squeaking on its hinges as she pulled it open. Her heart pounded at the sound, but she held it as still as she could as Blake and Brea entered the small room. She closed the door and, in the darkness, felt along the wall for the switch.

A dim bulb barely illuminated the room and Sarah bent down to move a few boxes, revealing a narrow, wooden trapdoor. "It's not been opened in a while," she whispered. "Cover your mouth and nose." She tugged at the door and dust clouded up.

"Who's first?" Brea asked. "I hate small spaces."

"Sarah first, then you, Brea. I'll keep an eye out and then join you."

Sarah climbed down the stone steps. The air was cold and smelt stale, the walls rough-hewn beneath her fingers.

A dull thud came from behind them and the last of the light faded. Blake shone the torchlight from his phone over their heads, as best he could under the low ceiling, and illuminated the space.

Christmas decorations lay in one corner and random objects littered the floor, all covered in a thick layer of dust. Chinks of

30

light shone down from the opposite wall. "It's here," said Sarah, crossing the space.

Brea rubbed her leg. "That's an awkward climb."

Blake wrapped his arms round her and kissed her forehead. "You'll be fine, promise."

"We could wait it out?" suggested Sarah.

"You said they have guns," said Blake, "so I wouldn't imagine they were dropping in for a cup of tea at 3 am."

Sarah ignored the sarcasm. "Why did they only attack when you arrived?"

"I think they're HexaMediCo. The three of us in one isolated place would be all their dreams come true."

"HexaMediCo?"

"Yeah," said Brea. "The root of all of this and why we think you, as Becca, disappeared. You were only supposed to be gone a short while but –"

They all stilled when they heard a shuffling noise overhead.

"There's at least one of the gunmen in the kitchen," whispered Sarah. "But when we pop out in the yard there might be more of them. What are we going to do?"

"I'll go first and stun anyone there. Literally." Blake grinned in the dim light, brandishing his gun. "Then you, Sarah. Brea, we'll help you out."

Blake opened the hatch to let in more light from the farmyard security lights and turned off his torch. He pulled himself into the chute and Sarah watched as he wriggled upwards, grateful she hadn't boarded the chute over in the cellar. The sounds of metal scraping came from above them, followed by a blast of cold air.

Sarah shivered but climbed up after Blake, ignoring the slippery, greasy texture of coal dust on her hands. At the top, a couple of flashes made her squeeze her eyes tight shut. When she blinked them open again, everything was in sharp relief, floodlights from the back of the house casting deep shadows across the yard. Blake had dropped to the ground.

She stifled the scream that formed by clamping her hand over her mouth, ignoring the coal dust on her tongue. Her breathing came faster and faster until a dizzying panic overwhelmed and even when she saw him roll over and scramble behind a barrel, the roaring pressure in her ears wouldn't subside. Another flash. Blake moved. He stood over something, stun gun pointed down. With a final kick, Sarah levered herself out the chute and approached. She froze. Someone was out cold on the ground.

"Go help Brea," said Blake, "and I'll make sure this idiot doesn't come around."

Sarah stared at the body.

"Sarah?"

"Is he... is he dead?"

"No, stunned. Help Brea. Now!"

Sarah turned on autopilot and walked back towards the cottage. She hadn't expected violence, despite the weapons. She didn't belong in this nightmare.

"Sarah! Duck!" Brea's voice sounded loud and clear in the night air. Still on autopilot, Sarah dropped to the ground. A blast beam lit the air above her head, where she'd just been standing. She looked across to see another of the attackers, his gun aimed at her, drop to the muddy farmyard floor.

She hauled herself to a sitting position, the world spinning. "Oh god, oh god, oh god."

"Give me a hand!" shouted Brea.

Sarah stumbled to her feet, helping Brea escape the hatch, before squatting back down again. It was all too much.

Brea hunched down beside her and rubbed her back in big, slow circles. "Take slow deep breaths. Between us, we've got this. Okay?"

Sarah gulped a lungful of cold night air and tried to think. Her head swam, and she felt Brea tugging at her arm.

"C'mon," said Brea. "We need to help Blake."

In the yard, Blake stood with the two stunned men at his feet.

"It's HexaMediCo," he said, pointing to their weaponry.

Sarah looked and saw a logo of nested hexagons, arranged like a target. Her blood ran cold and she started shaking. "I know that pattern, I'd recognise it anywhere. Only, I've never seen it before."

Before she knew it, tears were rolling down her face. "I just want to curl up in bed and pretend none of this is happening. Why are you even here?" Shoulders heaving, she furiously wiped her wet face with her sleeve and looked to see both Brea and Blake watching her. "Sorry. Just been a long day. What do we do now?" she asked in a small voice.

"It's okay, we understand," said Brea.

"Yup," said Blake. "Next, we avoid the other guns, get to the car and put some distance between us and them."

"The side of the cottage where we came out has a gate which leads to the front. Let me get external footage." Through her info-lens, images of each room of the cottage and the exterior were beamed to Sarah. Three men were inside, signalling to each other and creeping through the downstairs rooms, checking each one in turn. "There's no one outside other than us right now. Three men inside. I'll turn off the security lights, so we can't accidentally activate them. Keep the wall to your right as we go."

The three of them closely followed the contour of the cottage's wall down a dark alleyway, lined with trees on the other side. Sarah was convinced every shadow was another person with a gun, jumping at every perceived movement but they all reached the gate unscathed.

"It's locked," said Blake. "I can't open it."

"Fingerprint sensor," said Sarah. "Shit, I forgot. I never use the gate. No point really because the yard is wide open but..." She looked up to see the others in the dim light. "Sorry, I'm rambling. Let me past." She pressed her index finger to a dark panel mounted on the gate post, expecting it to light up and read her print. Nothing happened. "I can't get it to work but the tech system says it should. I can't override it either. We need to find another way out."

Brea shone a light from her phone onto the scanner. "Try again. Let's see what's happening."

Sarah tried each finger in turn, trying not shake in frustration and fear, but the sensor appeared dead.

"I think you've got too much coal dirt on your hands for the scanner to read your prints."

Sarah spat on her fingers and rubbed them on her jeans. "Is that any better?" she asked, pushing her hands under Brea's torchlight to check, unable to see the look of disgust on the others' faces. She pushed her index finger against the scanner again. With an audible click, the gate swung open to reveal the car a short distance away in front of the cottage.

# Seven

**4 am, 15ᵗʰ August 2035**

Sarah was jittery, despite the car being only a few feet away. She forced herself to calm down, and urged Brea and Blake forward, conscious that two men were still out cold in the yard. They weren't safe yet. She closed the gate, hoping the lock would confound their pursuers. A church bell tolled in the distance and broke through her thoughts.

"If their feed on the front of the cottage is live, we need to go. Now." Sarah's voice was loud in the night air and she startled herself with the sound of her own voice taking command.

"Okay, Sarah, back seat. Brea, passenger. I'll drive."

The indicator lights flashed on the side of the vehicle, far too brightly for her liking, as Blake unlocked it, and Sarah ran faster than she thought possible. The door was smooth and her fumbling fingers couldn't find a handle.

Brea arrived a second or two later, just as they heard shouts from the cottage's front entrance and the door rattling on its chain. Brea ducked and swung the car doors open with a quick, smooth motion. Sarah dived onto the backseat and peeked up to see two men with guns racing towards them. The men slowed and split, one heading each side of the vehicle. The sight laser from one of the guns reached into the body of the car, scanning. Sarah cowered down. This would be it. And she'd never know why.

Sudden acceleration threw her down in the seat, and another rolled her into the foot well. It hurt, her limbs twisted, and the speed prevented her from getting up, but she was alive, for now. They took the twisted country lanes at speed and Sarah spent time collecting her thoughts and working up into a sitting position, as they sped away.

The headlights weren't on and Sarah wasn't sure how Blake could drive so quickly with no outward visibility. When she looked over his shoulder, she could see the shape of the road superimposed on the inside of the windscreen. They were jerked from side to side and from bend to bend, as he pushed the car to its limits, but it got them away quickly.

They all sat in silence for a while. That was fine by Sarah. The past eighteen or so hours had turned her life on its head and soon her head lolled back, a mix of adrenaline and exhaustion forcing her eyes closed.

She woke with a start when the car slowed to a halt. Rubbing her eyes with the back of her hands, she looked out the window and tried to work out where they were.

She saw a generic, covered car park. Blake and Brea seemed more comfortable, which she took as a good sign.

"We're at our apartment," said Brea, looking nervously at Sarah. "I mean, the one the three of us shared. This'll be weird for us all, I guess."

"I've run scans and no one's been there since we left a few hours ago. We should be good to grab a shower and work out what to do next," Blake said as they crossed over to the lift access. He tapped his fingertips against the print scanner. Doors drew open and seconds later, they were whisked smoothly upwards.

Sarah was too tired to argue. She trusted the pair enough that she didn't think they'd try anything on, but uncertainty still buzzed at the back of her mind.

A short carpeted corridor led from the lift to the apartment. The building had an air of peace and Sarah imagined it was a quiet place to live.

"Try opening the lock," urged Blake, indicating the scanner.

Sarah shrugged and pushed her hands deep in her pockets.

"Sorry. Too soon?" Blake put his fingertips against the lock and with a light snick, the door opened.

The apartment was a conversion – an old mill or some such, Sarah judged – open plan, with original brick and steel beams, adorned with modern glazed panels and lighting. Sarah walked through, trailing her hand over the solid oak dining table, its tactile surface drawing her close. "That's gorgeous."

Blake pulled Brea into a tight embrace. Sarah didn't notice at first, too busy looking round at the apartment. Eventually, she heard the silence and turned towards them. "Is everything okay?"

A moment passed with no reply. Blake coughed, and Brea looked down at her shoes. "Um, yeah. It's just, you're so like Becca right now, it hurts. She chose the table because she loved the wood. She used to curl up on the seat right there to read and you're her but not her and…" Brea gulped a lungful of air. "I don't know what happened to you, but damn, I want what we all had back!"

Blake and Sarah watched as Brea ran from the room, disappearing behind a slammed door. They stayed quiet.

"What does she mean, what we all had?" asked Sarah, when enough time had passed she could look up at Blake.

"We were a throuple. Unconventional, I know, but it worked for us. And we called ourselves a 'hivemind' as our thoughts were connected when we wanted them to be. We miss that buzz between us. We shared this apartment together and despite you promising we'd stay together, you disappeared. Brea and I have spent the past few years trying to unravel what's happened and quite honestly, we'd about given up hope we'd ever see you again." Blake paused, staring into space. "If you'll excuse me, the

37

bathroom is through that door there and you'll find clean towels on the shelf. I need a few moments to check on Brea."

Sarah stood awkwardly as Blake knocked softly on the door that Brea had disappeared into. After a moment, he entered, the door closing behind him.

None of this helped answer the questions she had; that'd have to wait. She locked the bathroom door, grimacing at the smell of her clothes and herself as she stripped – a metallic adrenaline tang mixed with sweat and dirt.

Her eyes widened when she saw herself in the mirror. Her face was dark with soot from the old coal chute and streaked with the tracks of pale tears in direct contrast. Despite her farmstead, she thought she'd never been filthier.

She climbed into the bath and stood under the showerhead, letting it pour down a stream of hot water over her body, washing away both dirt and tension. Grey water whirled down the drain and she investigated several shampoos and body washes before finding something that smelt fresh and minty. Feeling more secure than she had done for the past day or so, she tipped her head back, massaging in the shampoo to let the foam build. The heat relaxed her shoulders and the constant stream of water helped clear her mind of everything she'd recently seen and done.

After a few minutes of bliss, Sarah opened her eyes to locate the body wash. A movement above caught her attention. She screamed. One of the ceiling panels had shifted and she found herself looking directly into the eyes of a man above her, crawling through the ceiling ducts.

Everything from there seemed to happen in slow motion. Her feet slipping in the bath. Jumping out, a mat saving her from sliding. The intruder crashing down. Him struggling to stand, tangling in the curtain, his shoes slipping in the wet.

Sarah pulled a towel and ran out the bathroom door, hastily covering her wet, bare skin. "Brea! Blake!"

"What's happening?" asked Brea, blastgun ready.

Sarah stuttered out a few words and pointed to the bathroom. Through the open doorway, they could all see the intruder getting to his feet. Blake strode towards the bathroom, blastgun in hand. The door shut behind him.

Brea lowered her weapon and put an arm around Sarah's shaking shoulders, leading her to the sofa. "Blake'll sort it. He always has done, since, well... Let's dry your hair." She grabbed a second towel and sat her down, slowly rubbing her mid-length hair whilst Sarah patted herself dry with awkward corners of her bath towel, trying not to expose herself.

A loud crack came from the bathroom, like something heavy had hit the sink. Both women winced, glancing at the closed door. After more noise, Blake stumbled out, grimacing. He used the wall for support, trying not to use his right leg too much as he approached the two women. "Well, glad to know I haven't lost my fighting skills."

"Oh?" asked Sarah, breathing out in long slow breaths to stave off the shakes.

"Yeah. I was taught to fight in prison in return for teaching what I know about counterfeiting." He looked over at Brea and Sarah, wincing again, as he opened the freezer door and rooted through for a couple of ice packs.

"Prison?" asked Sarah, frowning. Blake didn't seem the type to have committed a crime.

"Yeah. I suspect you disappearing was what I think triggered my release. I was no longer collateral."

He subconsciously rubbed the scar on his cheek.

Brea stood. "We can't stay here tonight now, well, what's left of it. I had a look up there and he was the only one, for now. There's no tech there, so I think this was fairly *ad hoc*. Let's find a hotel somewhere for a couple of nights to try and detangle this."

# Eight

**18th July 2031**

Becca chewed her lip nervously, watching the crowd gather. If her experiment were successful, it would really push the boundaries of humanity and save lives. In her mind, the possibilities were endless, from clearing landmines through to disaster rescue and relief.

She nodded politely to her father. She knew he was just interested in the intellectual side of the research. He'd buried himself in it ever since her mother died and barely spoke to anyone unless it was work-related.

Further along was Yates, the creepy Head of Security. She shivered as she watched him talking amiably to everyone there, from other research heads to the CEO. How he'd ingratiated himself like that, she didn't know. There was something about him that just made her skin crawl.

"Good to see you, Ms. Ford," Yates said.

"Doctor Ford," Becca corrected him. "Likewise."

"I'm glad to see your research move forward, there's so much potential application."

"Yes, the humanitarian aspects are enormous."

"Your research gives rise to so many more possibilities than that. If you really are successful in implanting extracted memories, every government and his dog will be clamouring for access. I'd be happy to act as your agent."

Becca frowned. "Agent?"

"I think we're about ready," interrupted Jona. "The droid shell is primed, and everyone is here."

"Thanks, Jona." Becca walked away, still frowning.

The Wetware Team gathered in the lab and Becca ran through their protocol and checklist for the last time. Two of the team would be in the ops room with the droid, ensuring the safe transmission of the data set. She and Jona would be in the lab, watching the various monitors the droid was hooked up to. Behind them would be the onlookers, able to watch both the data monitors and a live feed from ops.

The wetware interface was large and unrefined, still in development. It was wheeled in on a trolley and various wires hooked into ports in the droid's fingertips.

"Everything's in place here, Becca."

"Great. Stand back. I will start data transmission in three… two… one…" Becca keyed her code into the pad in front of her, following it up with fingerprint authorisation.

No one spoke. The room was silent. In ops, the interface box glowed, spewing forth a greenish haze as a semi-viscous fluid ran along the cabling, sealing the wires to the droid.

As it lay on the bed, the droid's eyelids opened, and Becca caught her breath, keeping a close watch on the digital outputs. Its eyes flickered from side to side, too fast for a human. A monitor beeped.

Instinct told Becca something was wrong. "Get out," she yelled into the mic to ops. "Get the fuck out. Now!"

There was a flash in front of the camera and thick smoke filled the view. Screams came through the mic. Jona started for the ops room but Becca caught their arm. "Don't. Please."

Becca typed in the droid override codes. The screams continued and Becca and Jona stared, open-mouthed, at the monitors. All outputs were erratic. The smoke didn't clear; they were working blind. In the background, Becca was vaguely aware of rising volume from the crowd. Yates strode forward followed by her father. "What's happening?" he demanded.

"We don't know." said Becca, irritation in her voice. "I'll tell you as soon as we do. Right now, I need to focus." She continued to type furiously but nothing suggested the droid had powered down. "I think the implanted memories have dislodged the overrides."

As the smoke cleared, they started to discern movement. A droid arm. A human face covered in blood. Nebulous images that cut in and out of view.

"I'm going in," said Yates, gun in hand. "Someone needs to take charge."

"Don't you dare," said Becca. "You do not have authorisation here. Get out!"

Yates lowered his weapon.

The smoke cleared. The room was unrecognisable from the clean, sterile space it had been. The bed frame was buckled and bent. The prototype wetware interface irreparably smashed. Blood splatters coated the walls and the two ops staff lay on the floor. One at an odd angle, not moving. The other still struggled and screamed under the droid, which had its hands gripped around the lab-tech's throat.

Becca slumped in her chair. "Please go and sort this, Mr Yates."

Still watching the camera feeds, she looked on in horror as he strode into the room, firing a bullet through the head of the still-twitching technician and then his colleague, before turning his attention to the droid.

# Nine

**6 am, 15<sup>th</sup> August 2035**

The three of them stood in the living area. Sarah self-consciously pulled her bath towel higher up, her damp hair twisted up into a second towel.

"What do we do then?" asked Blake. "They planted a spy here and damned if they're putting me in prison again."

"They know the farm location and that we've all made contact," said Brea, worrying at her lip with her fingers. "How long can you leave it until going back, Sarah?"

"I... I don't know. The chickens'll be grumpy but can be left a few days. There's a tap-fed water dispenser and the food will –" Sarah stopped. "Sorry, I'm overthinking. Too many odd things happening." She hitched the towel again. "What happened to my clothes?"

Blake grimaced, looking down at his hands. "I wouldn't go into the bathroom right now. There's some cleaning to do."

Brea stood. "Your room is exactly as you left it. Here, I'll show you."

"I thought Blake said we were a throuple," Sarah said. "Why separate rooms?"

"We all agreed having our own space was important. You used to stay up late working. I'm a morning person. We just found what worked for us. Here." Brea opened a door and stood, staring in.

Sarah hesitated at the threshold. "Are you sure I don't have a twin? That it's me?"

Blake came up behind them. "If you were to get your memories back, you'd know. I just don't understand how you took yourself so far away in your head. Your research was advanced, but you must have done some seriously experimental shit on yourself to do this parallel life thing."

Brea turned to Sarah, her eyes filling with tears. "You better bloody not have permanently lost Becca in there. I'd never forgive you – her – if she's gone forever."

"I'm sorry, I don't know what to say." Sarah took a deep breath and stepped into the room. It was painted in neutral colours with modern art prints on the wall, very similar to the prints at the cottage. Sarah crossed to the dresser and picked up a photo frame. Seeing herself with Brea and Blake on a sunny beach, the three of them happy together, ripped the air from her lungs. What had she done that she'd lost all her memories? Was the cube she found in the beehive the key to all this?

Her eye flickered. The info-lens sprang into life and Sarah gasped in surprise as it had only worked at the cottage before. Nothing happened when she looked at anything else in the room but if she focussed on the photo, there was a distinct lens glitch. Excitedly, she unfastened the clasps on the back of the frame. Garbled lettering on the back of the photograph swam in front of her eyes. The lens flashed and in her own handwriting she could now read, "Check the honey."

It made no sense and tears of frustration and disappointment welled. If she was going to leave herself clues, she hoped she'd be able to understand them. Sarah figured she might as well get dressed and join the others; something might spring to mind on the way. Her hands trembled as she pulled open the first drawer, feeling like she was snooping on a stranger. She grabbed the first set of underwear she could find and rummaged for socks and a t-shirt.

Five minutes later, she was dressed. The jeans she found were slightly loose – all that farm work, perhaps? – but nothing a belt didn't sort. The shoes were comfortable and broken in against her feet and a t-shirt and hoodie finished off the look.

She glanced in the wardrobe, curiosity winning out. A moulded plastic case caught her attention – it was branded with the same nested hexagon logo she'd seen on the guns earlier. She reached forward to trace the shape of it with her fingertips. It was so familiar, like a shape she'd doodled thousands of times in a previous life.

Standing in the doorway, she looked towards the living area. Blake and Brea were there, in a tight embrace. Taking a deep breath and waiting to ensure they weren't looking in her direction, she skipped over the hallway and into the bathroom. She needed to retrieve her cube.

Sarah clamped her hand to her mouth and nose as a rich metallic odour filled her nostrils. Blood spattered the walls; the corner of the sink was broken off, the mirror smashed. The shower head had been ripped off and the hose was now and the hose was now tightly wound around the neck of the man who'd crashed through the ceiling panel.. He lay at an odd angle, blood congealing from a gash in his forehead. She wondered what self-defence Blake actually knew, as he looked to be barely damaged in comparison.

She edged forward to get a closer look, noticing the all-too-familiar logo on his t-shirt. She knew he had a weapon – she'd seen it as he fell – but it wasn't visible now and she didn't want to get any closer to the corpse than she had to.

Careful not to touch the body or slip in any pooling blood, she pulled her jeans and shirt out from under the intruder's feet. Her clothes stank and were covered in mud, soot and dirt, and whilst she didn't like the idea of wearing someone else's clothes, Sarah was grateful to not have to get back into them.

The cube was still tucked securely in the front jeans pocket and she pulled her phone from her back pocket. It flashed with a message, causing her to frown. The last time she'd used it was when Blake had called and before that it was new out of the box. Had these people tracked her via her phone? She rubbed her forehead, standing motionless in front of the body as the confusion of the past few hours percolated through her brain. There had to be answers, but now people were dying, even if it was in self-defence. Her life had turned from an awful dream into a living nightmare.

Butterflies roiled in Sarah's stomach as she tried to connect the dots. She'd been setup by this hexagon company somehow. 'HexaMediCo' Blake had called them. They'd been watching her for a long time and the two B's turning up at her front door had set something in motion. Two B's... Three Bees, the cottage, her supposed sanctuary?

"Any idea how to dispose of a body, then?" asked Blake from the doorway behind her.

It was enough that something broke inside her. "I think they traced you back here via my phone. I'm so sorry, I mean, I know it's not my fault, well, I don't think so, but I really –" she burst into tears, her shoulders shaking.

Blake strode forward. "They already knew we were here, it's okay. This is bigger than you can understand, at least until we work out how to restore your memories." He paused. "Need a hug?"

Sarah nodded. He was tall and enveloped her with his arms. He was warm and comfortable and familiar and yet, having had no contact from another human being in – how long? – felt strange and alien. The physical contact alleviated her immediate stress and she relaxed enough to stop crying, her shoulders slowing their shuddering. It gave her a moment to clear her thoughts and she snapped back into herself, working on how to solve their current issue of a dead body.

She pulled away from Blake. "Okay, so we need to work out what to do with this," she said, waving vaguely at the corpse. "Or do we just leave it for that company to clean up?"

He looked at her and nodded. "That's not a bad idea. They can either confess to spying on someone in the shower after having hacked the building security, or pretend they'd never sent a lackey…"

Sarah stepped towards the head and took a couple of photographs with her phone.

"What are you doing?"

"Gathering evidence," she said. "We can prove something happened and it'll tell them, if they're really tracking my phone and its contents, that they underestimated us."

"You've become more badass since I last knew you." He grinned. "C'mon, let's sort out what we're doing."

# Ten

**20<sup>th</sup> February 2032**

Becca sat in one of HexaMediCo's interview rooms. It was a sterile space, designed for patient intake procedures and basic health checks. The walls were white and flat, with no windows, and the lighting was set into the ceiling tiles. The room gave her the heebie-jeebies now, despite having used it many times for its intended purpose. Brea and Blake had told her exactly what Yates, Head of Security, was capable of here.

She glanced at her phone; security had kept her waiting long enough. She jumped to her feet, preparing to leave and let Yates know he could play his games another time. The door didn't move. It appeared to be locked.

"Hey," she fumed. "What's going on?"

The door swished open in front of her and she stepped forward.

"You know there's no need to shout, Ms. Ford. I got held up," Yates said, as he stood in the doorway. He spoke in quiet, clipped tones.

Becca shivered. Just the way he pronounced 'Ms', letting the buzz slide on his tongue as he enunciated her name, was enough to fill her with nausea. "It's Doctor, not 'Ms'." She pressed her nails into her hand as a distraction from the situation. "And we've been through these questions before. I still don't, and won't, know the answers."

48

Yates walked into the small space, sitting on the chair opposite. "Doctor Ford, for the last time, I want to know what you know. Your father made it clear he wants to expand on your ideas for his research and I know you have your altruistic plans."

"My father?"

"Wake up, girl!" Yates stood up and slapped her hard across the face in one swift move.

Becca clutched at her cheek, hot underneath her hand. "I can't give you what you want. I erased the knowledge from my brain and the memcube is destroyed. You and I both know that much. The research is gone."

Yates towered over her, pulling her head back by her hair and holding his fingers round her jaw in a vice-like grip. "You're lucky your father said we weren't to hurt you too badly. If it were up to me, we'd get to the bottom of this very quickly."

Becca tried to free herself of his grip, but he dug his fingers in harder.

"I'd beat the memories back into you," he smiled.

"You know that's not how it works." Becca hissed the words through her clamped teeth. "And I don't know why you keep referring to my father." She thought for a minute, her mind blank. "I don't know who he is."

Yates dropped his hand and laughed. "Well, I can see you don't believe you're lying. But you're certainly not telling the truth."

Becca rubbed at her jaw and stinging cheek. "You know what I've done. You'll never be able to use my research because even I don't know or have it any more."

"We don't need you if we have your memcube." His grin made Becca shiver.

"You can't recover human memories to a droid shell. The last one went haywire after receiving a short data set." She pressed her lips together, resolute. "People died in the aftermath. You were there."

"All in the name of research. You're too soft, like your mother, and not as logical as your father. And, even if he can't see the full benefit of your work, I can. Memories are data and manipulating them is worth a lot of money to the right people." Yates turned and picked up the chair.

"We're done here." He paused in the doorway. "Mark my words, Doctor Ford, I'll be keeping a careful eye on you and your friends. Should you ever get even close to those research memories of yours, I'll know. And I'll be waiting. Next time, I might not be so forgiving, either."

Becca breathed a sigh of relief, collapsing forward in the chair. The heat and sting were fading from her cheek and after all the blackmail and injury to her partners, it seemed as though Yates was backing off, realising the research was irretrievably gone.

Toying with the idea of returning to the lab – much good that would do her – she had a sudden craving to go home. No one attempted to stop her as she headed through the security doors to the lift, which brought her to the imposing atrium-like concourse of HexaMediCo.

It was loud and bright, with echoes of conversation and the clatter of human activity, which made Becca's head spin. She stood, uncertain what to do next. Security at HexaMediCo had already broken Brea's leg in a faux mugging, and Blake was in prison, Yates successful in his false accusations. She couldn't put them through any more, not if she truly loved them. She needed to shake security off once and for all. Tears threatened to well up, but the thought that Yates might see, via one of his myriad cameras, meant she forced them down again. She wouldn't give him the satisfaction.

"Becca," someone shouted behind her as she headed to the street doors, her heart heavy. Their voice echoed into the space. "Hey, Becca. Wait up a second."

She turned to see Jona, one of the lab assistants, running towards her.

"Are you okay? You look like shit," they said, eying her up and down.

"Yeah, I'm fine, just shattered so I'm heading home on leave for a few days." She hated lying but who else would HexaMediCo hurt to get to what she used to know? And Jona would know the truth soon enough.

She'd be useless in the lab now anyway; the small team all had their own pockets of knowledge and didn't share. The company insisted on that contractually, to prevent the competition hiring staff out from under them and gaining an edge.

"Security wouldn't tell me where you were," Jona said, looking down. "But you left your notebook on your bench, which I thought was weird as you never go anywhere without it. It means you couldn't have left. Glad I caught you."

They held out the pocket-sized book to her. Becca took it and forced out a smile. "Thanks."

"As long as you're okay."

"I'm fine Jona, really. Just need some sleep and fresh air and I'll be right as rain."

Becca grabbed a cab and tried to formulate a plan. The car jostled her from side to side in the heavy traffic flow, and the headlights from oncoming vehicles flickered in the rain. She clutched her temples and willed herself to think.

At the door to the apartment she shared with Brea and Blake, it suddenly struck her she might never see it or her partners ever again. It was a wrench to her gut and she had to force herself to press her fingers to the scanner lock and enter.

"Hello?" she called into the darkness. "Brea?"

No answer. Satisfied she could work up an escape plan without interruption, she brewed coffee. As the water heated, she pulled the notebook out from her pocket. She knew it inside out: the paper itself was a luxury and the inscription on the inside cover was seared into her brain, as was the handwriting: 'To record precious memories, love Mum xxx'

51

Tears welled up and Becca sobbed. It wasn't fair. It wasn't fair that she had to lose everything to do what was right. She had to walk away from her home, her lovers, the job she loved doing. She had to, though, otherwise people would die at Yates' and HexaMediCo's doing, and their blood would be on her hands. She let the tears come, cascading down her cheeks in a release of grief she didn't know she'd been holding in. It was only when her eyes were puffy and red, that the crying slowed.

Becca took a few gulps of air and then sipped at her coffee. It was dark and strong, just how she liked, and she took it and the notebook to her desk, ready to get to work.

Once sitting, she hesitated. How could she just disappear? She idled through the pages of the book. Tucked in near the front was a photograph. It was a selfie of her, Brea and Blake, taken at St Bees, one of their favourite places to hang out in summer. She flipped it over and frowned, puzzled. 'No honey makes Becca funny,' was written in her handwriting just above 'St Bees, August 2031'. She couldn't remember writing it, though, which meant she must have written it before excising a set of memories.

Head whirling at this new idea, Becca realised how she could disappear. If she removed all traces of Becca from herself and created a new identity, she'd never be tracked down. Blake had shown her a few tricks for counterfeiting documents so perhaps she could really do this. Excitement bubbled up, and she found herself pacing in the apartment, thinking about who she could be and where she could go.

Becca stopped with a jerk and dashed to the kitchen. At the back of the cupboard of jars and sauces, she pulled out a jar of honey. She was the only one who ate it, so it would be the ideal place to hide something, wouldn't it?

Boggling round with a teaspoon proved she was right. Within seconds, she had a sticky memcube in her hands. Excitement grew as she rinsed it off and saw it was full of joined nodes and veins, full of... something.

She retrieved the memcube reader from her wardrobe and inserted the cube, and her hand, into the device. Her fingers, then her arm and then her whole body buzzed and vibrated with a weirdly familiar discomfort. The cube glowed, its contents crossing the barrier between digital and tissue.

Becca didn't know how much time had passed but she went and lay down on the bed, waiting for the nausea to pass. Thinking it through, she thought it shouldn't take long as she was restoring her own memory and it hadn't been gone for very long. As she waited, her brain reconstructed nodes and neural connections.

Becca's mind suddenly flooded with details of her research, how the wetware interface was constructed and how memory was digitised, removed and restored. And if Yates learned what she'd just done, she and her partners were all vulnerable.

Hoping there were no cameras or spyware in the apartment, Becca paced, fuelled by adrenaline. She needed coffee and ideas. Lots of ideas.

Becca didn't know how many times she could remove a set of memories and restore them without damage, but realised she might not have a choice. If she could delete her research from her mind, then insert a layer of false memory to become someone else, and finally remove Becca, she could totally disappear.

She sat up with excitement. If she became someone else, could she create temporary connections to fail once she'd completed a specific task? That way she could remove Becca and hide the memcube, forgetting she'd ever done so.

She spent several hours feverishly scribbling on her tablet, working out her multi-layered memory excision with temporary inserts. It was ground-breaking. Exactly what HexaMediCo wanted from her. But it was high risk. Brain impairment or lesions were possible and then she'd not be able to restore anything, ever. Brea and Blake would be permanently gone from her life. She looked up to see the photo of them all at the beach. It was bittersweet. She would have to build in some fail-safes, some clues, just in case. After another couple of hours, Becca stretched her arms and was startled to see the dawn light breaking. But, she had a plan and now had to put it into motion.

# Eleven

**7 am, 15ᵗʰ August 2035**

Back in the living area with Brea and Blake, Sarah realised she couldn't go on any longer without getting some answers. She hunched over in the armchair and looked over at the others. "I have questions."

Brea sank back on the sofa, her jaw tense. She sat up, crossed her arms and uncrossed them again before getting to her feet. "I know. But we need to get out of here. I'm scared."

"Me too, but you owe me answers," Sarah started, wondering what she was actually going to ask. "So, the bathroom intruder aimed a gun at me. Where is it now? It wasn't in the bathroom."

Blake pulled a device out of his pocket. "I've not seen one like this before but it appears to be an immobilisation device rather than a gun. It'll bind organic tissue and destroy everything else."

"Good," said Brea. "We might need a variety of weapons, and frankly after everything those bastards have done to us, they deserve anything we give them." Her jaw set and Sarah looked at her in admiration, discovering a core of steel in Brea.

"Okay, next question," Sarah said. "The hexagon logo. You recognised it, but it means nothing to me despite me having such a reaction. It was on the weapons of the men who attacked us in the farmyard. The dead guy has it emblazoned on his t-shirt. And, well, I saw it on a case in Becca's room. What the hell is this company?"

Brea sighed. "They're HexaMediCo. You work for them. Well, you did. You were their rising star." She glanced at Blake who inclined his head in agreement.

"Your research was on wetware – the interface between human biological memory and how it could be stored artificially. You reached a breakthrough when you found it worked both ways. Both storing and restoring it. Only someone at HexaMediCo wanted the tech for less than ethical or legal purposes. You found out that rather than helping trauma patients, they wanted to use it for political and financial influence. So you refused. And they didn't take no for an answer." Brea stopped, her gaze drifting into an empty space above Sarah's head, her eyes filling with tears.

"Yeah, it wasn't a good time." Blake said, reaching out for Brea's hand and squeezing it in reassurance. "I mean, we were all in agreement that they couldn't and wouldn't have their way, but we never thought you'd disappear on us. That was the low point." He looked down and massaged the bridge of his nose, shoulders shaking ever so slightly.

Sarah took in a deep breath. "Okay, so hypothetically, what would my stored memories look like?"

Brea leapt off the sofa. "Of course, the memcube!" She ran out, to return a few minutes later, holding a tiny transparent cube in the palm of her hand. The sparse network inside shimmered with gold veins.

Sarah held back her excitement, feeling her own cube press hard into her leg through the thin fabric of her pocket. Forcing her voice to stay even, she asked, "What's that?"

"It's a memcube – memory cube – the basis of your research. After they'd failed to blackmail you, hospitalised me and locked Blake up," Brea said, her voice shaking whilst she subconsciously massaged her leg. "After that, you dumped some memories on to this and asked me to hide it."

"And how does someone transfer their memories back?"

"We don't know exactly, but that case you saw? You, Becca, told us to keep hold of it. When we looked, it seemed to have a slot for a memcube that size."

"But, even if you were to use that, those memories still wouldn't make any sense, would they?" Blake said slowly, evidently thinking it through.

"What do you mean?" Brea played with her lip, disappointment dampening her previous excitement.

"When Becca gave you the cube, she was Becca. If Sarah restores whatever's on there, it'll feel like someone else's memories, not hers. There's a chunk of memories missing which connects Becca and Sarah. There's another cube somewhere."

"Okay," said Brea. "Let's think this through. Only Becca knew how to remove and restore memories. If she removed her research, she wouldn't know how to restore herself or implant a different person. We know she removed the research from her brain to force your release, Blake. But she was still Becca then. So, she must have restored her research at least once more to know how to become Sarah and then removed it again. Fuck."

"So, I must have removed and restored the original set multiple times. Is that what you're saying?" asked Sarah. "And that means there's a cube that will restore me to Becca, then one that will restore my research and then the mystery one that Brea has in her hand?"

"Yeah," said Blake. "I guess so. Or the cube that restores you to Becca also restores your research memories. Only I don't think you'd do that. You're more careful." He paused for a moment. "How about this scenario? You removed your research from your brain and hid it. HexaMediCo knew you'd done it so let you go to try and find it for themselves, or better still find you with it restored. Then you did restore it, made another couple of excision sets, creating multiple memcubes, and doing some dodgy experimental shit to your brain to help you hide them when you'd become Sarah."

"I wish to hell you'd told us what you were doing," Brea said, her voice low and quiet, glaring at Sarah. "I'd never have let you go like that. And the damage you've done to your brain. You always talked about the dangers of scarring, the, what do you call it, cortal interface, I think?"

They sat in silence. The cube in Sarah's pocket seemed to be boring a hole in to her leg. Guilt nagged at her but she still held back from mentioning it, leaving the other two in limbo. She was sure they were telling the truth but still, what if there was more to the story? She really wanted to regain her memories in private and work out who she was without relying on the word of the others. That had to be the next step. She thought back to what she'd seen when the cube activated back at the cottage. There were lots of tantalising glimpses of things but nothing that reminded her of work or research.

"Would it be possible to preview a memcube's contents?" Sarah asked.

"I dunno. I guess it might be, but only the owner of those memories would be able to make sense of any of it, from what Becca said of her lab's work."

"Okay," said Blake, standing up, suddenly. "We *really* need to leave. We can stay here all day but the longer we're here the more dangerous it feels. We can talk more in the car."

Sarah grabbed the case from Becca's wardrobe. She knew she had to use it. If only she could find some time to herself and get it to work with her cube, she could unravel the craziness of the past twenty-four hours and work out who and what she was.

She waited near the door for Blake and Brea, the thought of the cubes worrying her brain. From what she'd seen of the one in her pocket, that would answer the mystery of Becca, but there was still a question of the research. Unless Becca and the research were both on the cube she had. The one Brea had wasn't the research, she knew that much but something else entirely, predating everything else.

"Stupid question," she said, casually, to hide the glimmer of hope, "but do you have any honey?"

"Uh, yeah," said Brea. "You're. No, sorry, *Becca's* the only one that eats it and I don't think we chucked it out."

Blake reached up and pulled out a jar. "Here you go."

Sarah unscrewed the lid and thrust her fingers in, pushing them round. She pulled out a small, sticky object that left a trail across the counter. Rinsing it under the tap, she revealed another cube to Blake and Brea. One that looked denser than the one in her pocket.

"There was some writing on the back of a photo in the bedroom. My info-lens saw it." Sarah explained, heart racing. The difference in density of all three implied a different quantity or network of connections. If they were all her memories, perhaps she could work out the full story and go back to a nice, quiet life away from dead bodies and violence.

She was still deep in thought as they headed to the parking garage, leaving the apartment and the dead guy from HexaMediCo behind.

They climbed into the vehicle, Blake driving them into the early morning light. Despite questions, Sarah remained quiet, needing to process everything she'd experienced in the previous day or so.

# Twelve

**10 am, 15th August 2035**

Sarah was jolted from her thoughts when she recognised they were driving down into the bowl of a couple of low hills. Behind them, the sun cast shadows onto the wide sandy beach that stretched out before them.

"St. Bees," she whispered, amazed. "Part of the puzzle."

They all got out of the car and spent a few moments stretching. The air was cold against Sarah's face and the sea-salt tang filled her nose and lungs with deep seated familiarity. A few seagulls wheeled and screeched and, in the far distance, someone was walking their dog but otherwise it was quiet and empty. The tide was out, and the day was clear enough the line of the horizon looked to have a slight curve.

Sarah smiled. It was a far cry from the drama of the past day or so and the isolation and peace soaked through her whole body. Her shoulders dropped and the idea it might all be okay, that she'd be able to return to a normal life, whatever that was, sprang to mind.

First, though, she had to work out how to use the mystery device and see if it could tell her who she really was and work out why she'd snuck away from the people she loved, if it were true. They were her memories and she wanted to be alone when she recovered them.

She walked towards the public amenities block, the HexaMediCo case in hand, feeling with every step the weight of consequences the cube might bring about. The ladies' toilets smelled freshly cleaned and empty, too early in the day for tourists. Sarah locked herself into the largest cubicle and sat on the floor, the case positioned squarely in front of her.

She took a deep breath and popped the catches, the lid opening with a loud click. Most of the contents were moulded foam padding, precision cut to house a black, polished metal device. On the top was a small, inset cube-sized hole and when she pushed the fingers of one hand into a slot on the side, they fell into finger-sized smooth grooves. None of it was familiar but there didn't seem much to it; there were no switches or buttons, no slots or anything to indicate a mechanism. And surely, if she'd buried how to store memory, she'd make retrieval easy?

Listening for a moment to make sure she was alone, Sarah took the cube from her pocket. Under the halogen lights of the toilet block, the metallic veins glowed bright and remembering what had shone from it in the cottage – those few dizzying, disco ball moments of sights and sounds – she pushed it into the slot on the top, full of hope.

Nothing happened.

Palpable disappointment flowed through Sarah. She tried again, pushing her fingers back into the side slot. Squinting at it, hardly daring to open her eyes, she waited. For a few moments, the only sounds were her breathing and outside, the seagulls squawking as they wheeled across the bay.

Then, something flowed round her fingers. It was warm and viscous, a gel-like substance that moulded to her hand, gluing it into a precise position, one finger at a time, and finally, her thumb. Sarah tried not to panic, knowing she was fully connected to the machine. "Too late to back out," she muttered, in between breaths. "Guess this is supposed to happen."

The cube started glowing and the brighter it got, the more her fingers started itching, then buzzing. The sensation built through

61

her fingers, up through her wrist and started up her arm. Sarah sat still, trying not to clench her jaw as her whole body vibrated. In her mind she visualised her entire nervous system fusing with the memcube device. Her stomach flipped as though she was about to vomit and then, there was a pause. She gulped in big breaths of bleach-tainted air and tried to sink into all the weird feelings. Needle-pricks twanged at all her nerves.

Just as she started relaxing into the sensation, the buzzing ramped up to an intensity that made her clutch her forehead tight with her other hand. It sang through her sinuses and teeth; her ears were clanging and the room spun and spun until it no longer existed. But then, snatches of memory drifted by, too fast to catch, but there was laughter. Human touch. Celebration. Sadness. A brief smell of perfume she knew Brea wore. A glimpse of a party. Hers. A laboratory late at night. Everything flowed in a relentless three-dimensional stream of consciousness. It was beautiful and ugly, strange and alien and totally belonging to her. They were her memories. Becca's.

The gel-like substance subsided as though it never existed. Sarah sat for a few minutes, feeling wobbly. Her fingers were intact, the skin smooth and unpunctured. When she examined the cube, it was empty. She replaced the device, closed the case and pulling herself up the wall, wobbled to her feet. Outside, she saw Blake and Brea, sat on the edge of the sand. She smiled. They always did make her smile. The three of them were good together.

She walked over and sat down. "I lied to you. I found the second memcube. I restored it."

"We wondered what took you so long," said Brea. "But just thought you needed some time – wait! How do you feel? Who do you think you are?"

"I'm Sarah. But Becca. Both at the same time, it's so confusing. And I think... I think, I need to be sick..." She keeled forward, feeling her two partners drop to the sand with her.

Someone held her hair back, and the other stroked her back in slow circles.

"The night I cut you off when you wanted to find out about the surveillance? The cottage tech system sensed the proximity of the cube and after scanning my fingerprint it triggered a preview. It's why my instinct said to trust you. In all the chaos it showed, in those few seconds, somehow I knew." Bile rose in her throat. "Oh god. I really am going to heave."

"You're bound to feel grim," said Blake. "You've just shocked your head in so many ways."

On all fours, her memories mingling and settling: the dual knowledge of her existence, the sensations the memory device had thrown at her, all coalesced and she heaved, sharp bile flooding her mouth. A moment later she vomited hard into the sand and everything went fuzzy round the edges. The sky spun and screams of the gulls pierced her head. Supported by Brea and Blake, she passed out, overwhelmed.

# Thirteen

**11 am, 15<sup>th</sup> August 2035**

Becca woke up. Her bones ached, and her shoulders were stiff. Looking round from her prone position on cold, dry sand, she stifled a happy cry. Brea and Blake sat next to her, chatting quietly. One of them had put a coat over her sleeping body, waiting for her to come round.

"Hey, sleepy head," said Blake.

Becca rolled over and sat up, wiping grains of sand off her sleeves and out of her hair. She looked at both of her partners and grabbed them in a huge hug.

"Urgh, you stink," laughed Brea, brushing hair back off Becca's face, her fingers lingering for longer than necessary.

Becca laughed back, pressing Brea's warm hand to her cheek. "How long was I out for?"

"About half an hour," Blake said. "But we've seen you sleep after memory restoration before, so we knew we just had to wait."

He pulled his arm tight around Becca's waist and she sank into his embrace.

"What do we do now?" asked Becca. She spoke slowly, frowning as she worked things through. "We're now back to where we were when I disappeared but have two cubes with some of my memories stored. One looks like it's my research, from what I remember of the density. The other, I don't know."

"I just don't understand how you became someone else, though," said Brea, gripping both partners' hands tight.

"As well as removing real, existing memory, I figured it might be possible to implant false memory. So, I used what Blake taught me, plus a few other tricks and created a new identity, taught myself farming and self-defence –"

"Ha! You know Kung-fu!" said Blake, eyes twinkling, knowing the others would get the joke.

Becca flushed. "Well, yeah. That may have been some of the inspiration for the ideas. Anyway, I hacked my way round to gather the money I needed and like that – poof – I was gone!"

"Okaaaay," said Brea, worrying at her lip. "But that still doesn't explain how you knew to hide the cube at the farm, once you were Sarah."

"Well, I planted temporary –"

"It does explain how Becca had paid for a year's rent in advance, though," Blake said, interrupting her. "I always wondered how that happened."

"Shhh!" Brea mock-glared at Blake, squeezing his hand again.

"Okay. I planted clues for myself in the hope they would be enough to push me in the right direction, should they ever be triggered."

"Huh? You said that wasn't possible because it'd cause too much disruption to the neocortex."

"I know," replied Becca. "Truth is, I didn't know it would work, I just had to make a best guess. Obviously it did, because I'm here."

"And have you damaged yourself?"

Becca pursed her lips. "I don't know. It's highly likely. When Blake asked about the beehive, it set off a kind of physical alarm in my head, which I wired in via manipulating a few nerve clusters. There's likely to be some scarring at the very least, as it's not my speciality."

"But why, Becca, why did you go?" Tears welled up in Brea's eyes. "We were a team, dammit. We agreed to stick together. You *promised*."

"But I had to. I hated that you were interrogated and blackmailed. And hurt! I don't know who's in charge of HexaMediCo, but I wish I could make them pay for what they did to you both. To us… What?"

Brea and Blake were staring at her wide-eyed.

"What do you mean you don't know who's in charge?" Blake asked, looking confused.

"Why should I?" demanded Becca. "All I know is that they, along with that bastard Yates, threatened the people I love the most and caused all this heartache and grief."

"I think we've found the contents of the other cube," muttered Blake. He spun his head round at a noise behind them. "Well, well, they must have been following our car after all."

Footsteps approached, well-heeled shoes tapping out a steady rhythm on the concrete steps and a second, quieter pair. The three of them turned.

Becca groaned. "Yates. He did threaten he'd always be watching. And is that the CEO? Guess they've been tracking us all along in the hope of getting their grubby mitts on my research. At least I can let them know how I feel."

Brea elbowed her to get her attention. "Yeah, that's Professor Ford. If anyone will listen to you, it's him."

"Good," said Becca, glaring. "I want to put an end to all of this."

"No, you don't understand. *Ford*. Your surname? That's your father."

Becca examined the man in front of her. His bearing suggested self-belief, entitlement, someone used to giving the orders. Greying round the temples but with an improbably smooth complexion that meant it was impossible for her to guess his age. He wore no glasses, but the tell-tale flicker of his eyes showed her that, like herself, he wore a lens implant to provide him with information at any given time. Becca's info-lens only worked in close proximity with the cottage tech, so she found his disconcerting to watch, as his eyes constantly roved in different directions.

"Ah, Rebecca. It really is you. When Mr Yates told me he'd found you after all this time, I had to come and see for myself." The professor nodded, standing back to look at them all. "And Breanna and Blake, of course. The three of you, always so happy together."

"What do you want?" asked Becca, her jaw stiff, as she battled between confusion and anger.

"You look and sound just like your mother." He smiled briefly, gazing out as though stuck in a past moment. "I see you've kept your promise."

"Promise? I don't even know you!" Becca clenched her fists.

"Exactly. You promised to disown the family name and expunge all memory of me if I didn't stop trying to persuade you to hand over your research. It always did seem a drastic move, but you do have your mother's fierce empathy."

"If that's true, I absolutely would have done it." Becca moved to stand in front of Brea and Blake. "You hurt the people I love most in the world. Of course I'm not going to –"

He held up a hand and Becca fell silent. "Your research is important to me, you know that. Together we could have worked out what it actually means to be human. You and I were to close to stabilising human memory into droid shells. Think what that future could bring."

"Brea was physically hurt and Blake was attacked in prison and he was only there because you put him there," Becca spat. She paused for breath. "My response isn't dramatic or 'fiercely empathetic', it's human. *Human.* Not a memory transplant without context or emotion. My research would get people killed. I wanted it to help people in disaster zones, not sell memories to the highest bidder."

The professor tilted his head. "Attacks? Blackmail? I know we had a few heated rows about your research, but violence?" He slowly spun to look at his security chief.

Becca stifled her tears. Neither those or the explosive anger she felt would help right now. "Yates!" she screamed. "He did all this. And you let him. You let him blackmail us. You let him injure Brea and lie to a judge to get Blake jailed. All for what?"

She was so focused that she jumped when warm hands gripped both of hers, realising only then how tightly she'd clenched them. She unfurled her fists and gave both Brea and Blake a squeeze back.

"Rebecca, please. This wasn't me. Of course I want your research, your work is truly outstanding, but violence is never an answer. We're more evolved than that."

Becca rolled her eyes.

"Can we go for a walk, just the two of us? See if we can work out what has happened." Without looking back, the professor strolled down the promenade.

Becca shrugged. "What choice do I have?"

She followed, catching up with him. They walked for a few minutes in silence until the professor stopped to look out across the bay.

"It's a lovely view," he said, reaching out to her until his fingers curled round Becca's wrist.

"It is," she agreed, breathing in the sea air, still furious. In the calm of the bay, the sun shining down, everything seemed a million miles away.

The professor rapidly tapped a rhythm against both the median and ulnar nerves at the top of Becca's wrist.

She blinked, her info-lens showed scrolling lines of code at a dizzying speed and all of a sudden, she was jerked out of her body, floating above herself and looking down.

"Are you there, Romeo-twenty-ten?"

Becca's vocal chords twisted, her lungs filling of their own accord and then her voice, "Yes, Professor."

"How many memcubes do you know are in existence?"

"Two."

"What memories do they contain?"

"One is unknown, the other is my research."

"I know you don't think much of me, but I do love you, Rebecca." The professor stared out to sea and blinked away a few tears. "End routine."

Becca shook her head, she'd zoned out for a moment, damned if she knew why. "Oh, yes, you're right, it is a lovely view."

"Well, Rebecca, you might have disowned me but I'm glad to have spent a few minutes with my daughter." The professor turned and walked back to where the others waited.

Becca followed, still uncomfortable with her body. Her info-lens glitched a few times and she frowned. It shouldn't be reacting at all this far from home.

"Now I know the memcube of Rebecca's research exists, I'd like to know where it is," said Professor Ford.

Becca's eyes widened. They'd only talked about the view. At the back of her mind, was a buzzing sensation, manifesting confusion, separate from her own thoughts.

Blake stepped forward. "It's at the farm."

Becca stared him down, mouth gaping at his audacious lie. "Why are you telling him this?"

"Because I know exactly where it is. Trust me."

The professor chuckled. "Well now, this is an interesting situation, isn't it?" He nodded at Yates. "Take the two girls in my vehicle. Blake will drive me, I'm sure. And splitting up the party will ensure less chance of trouble." He looked pointedly at Yates. "From anyone."

Becca folded her arms. "I'm not going anywhere."

Brea stepped forward, kicking up the sand in protest. "And neither am I."

"I don't think you have a choice, girls." It was the first thing Yates had said. The barrel of a pistol was just visible to them but out of sight of the others. "Professor Ford wants what he's owed. As do I. Best do as you're told."

"Go," said Blake. "We've got this. The three of us buzzing together again. Our hive mind."

Becca stared at him. "I don't know what you're doing but I don't like it."

Blake winked and grinned.

# Fourteen

**1 pm, 15th August 2035**

Tears welled in Becca's eyes and she blinked them back, breathing in hard to hold her stomach in and stop it from churning. Her head hurt with both Sarah's and Becca's memories overlapping and enmeshing, her brain reconfiguring. The past few years, her effort to save her boyfriend and girlfriend, it was all for nothing. And now they were trapped in a car with gun-toting Yates in charge.

Brea grabbed her hand, holding it tight. "You okay?" she whispered.

Yates glared at them in the rear-view mirror. "Shut it. I don't trust any of you. More fool Professor Ford for letting this drag on so long."

Brea glared back. "I hope he knows your opinion of him. Besides, what are you going to do right now? You don't have the cube."

"What's Blake playing at?" Becca whispered, as quietly as she could, her lips barely moving.

*I don't know. I'm scared.*

"Me, too," said Becca, suddenly realising that although she'd heard Brea's voice, Brea hadn't spoken aloud. It was a buzz at the back of her head. Yet, she'd heard her and replied, hadn't she? *Hive mind?*

More silence followed until finally, they drew up to Three Bees Cottage. Becca started walking round to the farmyard at the back of the cottage.

Yates grabbed her arm and pulled her round. "Where the hell do you think you're going?"

"I need to feed the chickens," she said, wriggling free of his grip. She strode off, glancing back to see Yates following a few feet behind, looking very unhappy.

Brea kept up with Becca, asking questions about the day to day working of the farmstead and helping collect the eggs. "I can see why this life suited you. I mean, suits you. Oh hell, I don't know what I mean, but it's a good life with fresh air and all this quiet and space."

Becca smiled and pulled her close, feeling the warmth of her body pressed against hers. She glared at Yates daring him to say anything. "When all this is over, we can all move in here, if that's what we agree."

Brea grinned. "I'd like that." She reached to give Becca a quick kiss on the lips. "Not so sure about Blake, though."

The sound of a car pulling into the driveway grabbed their attention.

"Come on," said Yates, waving the gun at them.

Becca signalled the cottage to let them in and soon they all stood in the front room. Yates following last, closing the front door with a firm click. The room was exactly how Becca might have left it: tidy and not as though there'd been a squad of intruders running through only the previous night. Clearly HexMediCo's goons had cleared up after themselves.

The professor looked round. "Well, Rebecca, you've certainly done well enough for yourself. I guess I'll deduct what you skimmed from HexaMediCo from your inheritance."

Becca smiled as she saw Blake's mouth drop. "That was the source of the money?"

She shrugged. "Guess so."

Yates paced, his gaze darting suspiciously between everyone.

Becca frowned, he was like the proverbial cat on a hot tin roof. What was he up to? He had a gun, but did he have any other surprises in store? The back of her head buzzed and she felt herself repeat the gun information, internally. *Hive mind?*

"So," said the professor. "Rebecca's research. Where is it?"

Blake, turning to face Becca, said, "If you had a choice of destroying your research or letting it out into the world, what would you choose?"

"Quit stalling." Yates reached into his pocket, gun clearly in hand.

The professor put his hand on Yates' shoulder. He spoke with a quiet confidence. "Put the gun down. We'll get the research and then negotiate between just the two of us."

"Becca?" prompted Brea.

"I'd burn it to the ground and stamp on its grave." Becca said, more vehemently than intended. "I'd give anything to see it gone."

Blake smiled. "But you'd also want to glimpse it, *preview* it, for even just a few seconds, wouldn't you?"

Becca hesitated. "I, I don't know." The buzzing in her head grew louder, *say yes.*

"Oh," chimed in Brea, her eyes lighting up as she inclined her head very slightly at Blake. "Imagine experiencing it, those totally immersive memories for just one last time?"

"What are you playing at?" said Yates, shrugging off the professor and stepping forward, waving his gun so they could see the loading lights on its side turn green. "We don't have time for this nonsense. Where's the research?"

Becca kept her face straight, she now knew what Blake was scheming. If they could pull it off, they'd be free. She backed into the corner of the room, next to her desk. From there, she had a clear line of sight of everyone. Reaching back, so slowly as not to be noticed, she ran her fingertips underneath her desk to activate the tech system. It silently booted into observation mode: the keyboard and display remained off, as she'd programmed with

73

that pressure combination. The monitor and sensors would wait for another input before appearing.

"Okay," Becca said. "A final preview it is." She turned, cube in hand, anticipating the position of the keyboard's fingerprint sensor, fingers also ready.

**Storage device detected.**
**Scan fingerprint to activate.**

The message had barely flashed when the room illuminated with fragments of speech, images of scribbled notes and lab experiments.

Everyone turned around, amazed by the dizzying, fragmented whirlwind of sound and light. Becca wanted to take it all in, bathe in her knowledge and use it for altruistic purposes. But she knew HexaMediCo, Yates, would twist and deform it. She really didn't know about her father.

The professor turned around and around, as though viewing everything he could. Yates did the same, looking up and down, left and right, in a methodical manner, his eyes flickering quickly enough to resemble a seizure.

Lost in the swirling array of moving images and bodies, Becca almost missed Blake's actions. She ducked and rolled to the side just as he fired the weapon he'd claimed from the bathroom attacker. A thick beam of light shot out, hitting the suspended cube square on and then wrapping round it, again and again.

Simultaneously, Yates whipped round, firing at Blake. The sound was explosive. Everything suddenly sounded far away interspersed with a roaring, rushing noise. Blake clutched at his chest and fell to the floor. Brea barrelled across the room and knelt down next to him, Becca only a second behind. From his position Blake grinned and winked up at them. *Bulletproof vest*, Becca heard in her head above the rushing. Where the hell did he get that from?

The walls of the room glowed brighter and brighter until the light shattered into myriad fragments casting rainbows everywhere. The light beams from the gun worked on the fragments over and over until Becca's desk was covered in a fine veneer of crystalline dust.

Silence filled the room. Becca looked round. The professor stood open-mouthed. Yates shook with silent rage. No one spoke.

Yates spun on his heel and slapped Becca hard across the face. "You stupid bitch!"

He turned to the professor. "Where can we get another copy?"

Becca clutched at her face, grinning. This was it, the home stretch. "You can only do so many extractions before there's scarring. That's common knowledge. Any more and I'd lobotomise myself. He," she nodded at the professor, "knows that."

Ford straightened up his jacket, also looking crestfallen. "She's right. She confirmed earlier there was only one copy. We just saw it turn to sand." He looked at Becca with disgust. "All this. All this wanting to save people and sacrifice no one. Think how much we could have gained by combining our research. We could make a better human race and reach the stars."

"It wasn't worth the expense," Becca whispered, tears welling. "People would die. If not at your hand, then at Yates'."

"You should have trusted me," said the professor.

"Why? I thought you were behind everything. I thought you were threatening our lives, which is why I cut you out."

"Well, you're safe now. Your research is gone." He walked to the door and turned back. "You may think you've succeeded, Rebecca, but you are carrying two concurrent memories. And one of those is a considerably long time since its extraction. I'm fascinated by both these aspects and will be watching your progress with very close interest."

He walked out, his shoulders slumped, seeming diminished, defeated. A stab of something hit Becca, but it was one visceral feeling pitted against everything else.

He turned back. "Mr Yates, let's go. We may be able to create some of the data back in the lab."

With the professor out of sight, Yates lunged at Becca, gripping her throat and driving her back against the wall. His eyes were wide and unfocussed. He leant in. "For your own sake, you better have just destroyed everything. I'll be watching you so closely I'll know every time you scratch your own nose."

The edges of Becca's vision blurred, and she slumped forward, gasping for air. Her ears drummed, drowning out everything else. In her fog she saw Brea, in slow motion, hurl herself at Yates and drag on his arm. Blake shouted something.

Yates laughed, dropping Becca. He turned to Brea and Blake. "I already shot you once," he hissed, through gritted teeth. "You should be dead."

He aimed his gun at them and backed to the door. "You'll never be safe from me. Every damn move you make, I'll know it."

Becca stayed in her position on the floor, hurting and exhausted. Raising her head, she could see her father and Yates standing next to the car, appearing to be in conversation. She blinked a few times using the info-lens to access the house-tech, enabling Brea, Blake and herself to eavesdrop on their conversation.

The professor caught Yates' wrist and the security chief stiffened, almost robot-like.

"Please hand over any weapons you're carrying, Yankee-eight-four."

"Yes, professor."

"Did you capture all the sounds and imagery?"

"As much as I could, professor."

"Good. We'll work on salvaging what we can once we're back at my lab." The professor shook with anger. "And I'll work on a new routine to reprogram your abilities to be less violent. We're supposed to be human, better than animals. And remember, you're my droid, not a free agent. You signed the contract yourself. End routine."

Yates shook his head like he'd just been daydreaming. He opened the passenger door for his boss.

"And perhaps we should drop in on Sierra-twenty-twelve for a progress update. She is almost on our route and we've not physically checked on her in a while."

Becca watched the car drive off and laughed. It was over! They were free at last. She'd relisten to that last conversation when her body wasn't full of exhaustion and adrenaline. Right now, she just wanted Brea and Blake in her arms.

Her phone beeped a message alert and she frowned at the noise.

*I know you were listening in just then, Ms. Ford. Shame you haven't learnt to override your internal program like I have. I can't be deprogrammed, only enhanced. Be seeing you.*

Becca remained on the floor. *Internal programming? But that would mean...*

"Thank goodness your brain was on form enough to hear me back when I worked out a plan," said Blake.

"What do you mean?" Becca frowned.

"Side-effect of your research," said Brea. "You did hear it, didn't you?"

Becca thought back to the buzzing in her brain and smiled. "Yeah, guess I thought you were being figurative when you said, 'hive mind'. Where did the bulletproof vest come from?"

"Your father took your words to heart and asked me about Yates in the car. He looked up what I told him, and every detail correlated, so he suggested I used one of the company vests stashed in the boot. Damn glad he did."

"Sounds like Yates won't be around much longer then," said Brea. "Thank the deities for that!"

Becca sat upright. "I don't know. I... I..." She dropped back to the floor and cried, holding Blake and Brea close.

# Fifteen

**8 am, 20<sup>th</sup> September 2035**

Daylight streamed in through the curtains, waking Becca up. Blake and Brea were still asleep, so she carefully climbed out of bed and tiptoed downstairs.

It was a beautiful late summer's morning, and the kitchen air soon filled with the smell of coffee as Becca brewed it. She flung the back door open, standing in her dressing gown and facing into the light.

She smiled. Her body was still loose and warm from sleep and the hens were busy clucking in their pen. A light wind blew, bringing the freshness of a new day.

She poured herself a coffee and stood on the doorstep again. Life was good.

"Hey, gorgeous," said Blake, kissing her shoulder and pulling her back into his arms.

"Hey." Becca tipped her head back against his warm chest and marvelled at how easily they'd fallen into a routine again. One that suited all three of them.

"Is there coffee for me?" called Brea, still wiping sleep from her eyes.

"Of course," Becca poured another couple of mugs, giving Brea a kiss. She took their drinks outside. As she put them on the table, she scanned the property via her info-lens. It was a new, daily habit, even with their upgraded security. But nothing had disturbed their peace since Ford and Yates had left.

At first, they'd huddled in the cottage, living in fear of retaliation, but over time they'd begun to relax. Country life suited Brea and even Blake complained less and pitched in more. They were both able to work remotely and between the three of them, they shared a comfortable life with fun and laughter, just like they used to. The spare bedrooms had been decorated, the dust cloths stored in the cellar and they quickly found a new routine.

Every so often, Becca would glance back at the memcube on the kitchen sideboard. She knew what it contained – Brea and Blake had told her – but she wasn't ready. Not yet.

She knew when she excised her father from memory she'd removed memories of her mother as well. Tears had poured down her face at the time, but it was worth it to protect Brea and Blake.

It hit her most just before she became Sarah, running her fingers over the precious notebook inscription for the last time, knowing the paper trail would be the only memory of what once was. She tucked it safely away in the apartment, hoping it would always be kept safe.

Now, it was her most prized possession, kept in her bedside drawer in the cottage and accessible at any time to sit with and meditate. Perhaps, one day, she'd restore the memories of her father. Just not now.

It was only when she allowed herself to think of his last mysterious words, 'Sierra-twenty-twelve' that her sinuses itched. There was a familiarity, but, it was too much to think about after everything that had happened. And she'd dismissed the crazy talk about droids. She knew who she was.

"Penny for them?" asked Brea.

"Nah," said Becca. "Hey, if the weather stays like this, fancy going to the beach?"

# About the Author

**Emma K. Leadley** (they/she) is a UK-based speculative fiction writer and queer, creative geek. They've had over 30 pieces of flash fiction and short stories published by independent presses, including Eerie River Publishing, Bag of Bones Press and Fox Spirit Books. *Telling the Bees,* from NewCon Press, is their first published novella and they have several more in the pipeline. Emma lives in Nottingham and regularly argues with their rescue greyhound for space on the sofa. They can be found online at autoerraticism.com.

## A huge thank you to:

Mike, for huffing and puffing over your hieroglyphics all those years ago which prompted me to start writing.

Laurie, for improving the science bits and being such a huge champion of my words. You are the shiniest of shiny crows.

The Semi-Feral Goblins and Team Stabby. I love you all, you wonderful humans!

My beta readers for taking a chance on my weird tale and encouraging me to make it the best it could be.

My Auntie Jo, and both my grandmothers. I'm sorry you're not able to see my writing in print but I'll be forever grateful for you teaching me a love of words and books and knowledge.

Alex Davis, for being such a constructive editor of the original story. And for running such useful events for writers that really get my creative juices flowing.

And last, but not least, Ian Whates for taking a chance on my lockdown, weird-COVID-dream inspired story and editing with such dry humour and empathy.

Hold on... if you're reading the acknowledgements page, it means you've probably read this novella. So, thank you to you too. (If you like it, please tell your friends about it. Or better still, buy them their own copy!)

# ALSO FROM NEWCON PRESS

### Best of British Science Fiction 2022 ed. by Donna Scott
Editor Donna Scott has scoured magazines, anthologies, webzines and obscure genre corners to discover the very best science fiction stories by British and British-based authors published during 2022. A thrilling blend of cutting-edge and traditional, showcasing all that makes science fiction the most entertaining genre around.

### Night, Rain, and Neon edited by Michael Cobley
All new cyberpunk stories from the likes of Gary Gibson, Jon Courtenay Grimwood, Justina Robson, Louise Carey, Ian MacDonald, Simon Morden, Gavin Smith, DA Xiaolin Spires. "Three hundred pages of thought-provoking cyberpunk that will give many hours of pleasure." – *SF Crowsnest*

### Sparks Flying – Kim Lakin
First ever collection from critically acclaimed author Kim Lakin, spanning fourteen years of writing. Her very best short stories, as selected by the author herself. Fourteen expertly crafted tales that span myth, science fiction, industrial grime and darkest imagining.

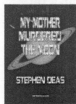

### My Mother Murdered the Moon – Stephen Deas
A tense mystery of sabotage and murder with far-reaching repercussions set upon a small space station orbiting Saturn's moon Epimetheus. Roxy took this job to escape her past, specifically to escape her mother. That's hard to do, however, when every feed from Earth is dominated by news of her mother's trial for mass murder.

### Salt on the Midnight Fire – Liz Williams
Remember that sense of wonder when first reading a truly magical book? Rediscover it in the pages of Liz Williams' Fallow Sisters novels. Bee, Stella, Serena, Luna: Four Fey Sisters whose lives straddle the contemporary and the 'otherworld' – skipping from current day London and rural Somerset to the past and alternative realms.